THE FIRST HUMAN RIDER

THE FIRST HUMAN RIDER

DRAGON APPROVED™ BOOK ONE

RAMY VANCE

MICHAEL ANDERLE

L M B P N

DISRUPTIVE IMAGINATION

Thanks to the Beta Readers
John Ashmore, Kelly O'Donnell

Thanks to the JIT Readers

Billie Leigh Kellar
Misty Roa
Kelly O'Donnell
Deb Mader
John Raisor
Diane L. Smith
Micky Cocker
Larry Omans
Dave Hicks
Angel LaVey
Jackson Hendricks
Jeff Eaton

If I've missed anyone, please let me know!

Editor
The Skyhunter Editing Team

LMBPN Publishing
PMB 196, 2540 South Maryland Pkwy
Las Vegas, NV 89109

First US Edition, December 2019
Version 1.02, February 2021
ISBN (ebook) 978-1-64202-669-6
ISBN Print: 978-1-64202-766-2

DEDICATION

This book is dedicated to Wee John!

—Ramy Vance

*To Family, Friends and
Those Who Love
to Read.
May We All Enjoy Grace
to Live the Life We Are
Called.*

— Michael

CHAPTER ONE

The old wizard stood over a boiling cauldron. Myrddin felt older now than he had in some time, although he wasn't sure if he looked it. In the reflection, he could see his hair hadn't grayed more and his skin hadn't wrinkled further.

The side-effects of being immortal, he mused.

The cauldron was roughly half his height, made of pewter, and its feet were clawed like dragon's feet. They were real dragon's feet, in fact, and they served as an anchor for the large bowl.

And that was exactly what Myrddin needed right now: an anchor.

He leaned over the cauldron and heaved a heavy breath as if he were trying to empty his entire body of the air inside, exhaling all of his fear and worry. He gripped the sides of the cauldron, the heat not affecting his magic-enhanced hands, and peered into its depths.

The water of the cauldron was dark and murky. Shapes moved but had no definition. Faces formed slowly out of the shadows and things began to move in the darkness—thousands upon thousands of creatures.

At first only orcs. Then goblins. Then trolls and drow and all manner of dark creatures. They were marching to meet another force—that of elves, dwarves, and halflings.

Then finally, humans.

As the forces of light banded together, Myrddin saw they were armed and marching toward a bright red light in the distance. He could even hear the screams. Everywhere.

He felt the heat from the red light and knew what he was watching: the armies of the Dark One.

Something behind Myrddin moved. The wizard turned and whipped his wand out, pointing it at the shadows behind the door. When he looked out of the window to his left, he saw shadows that could not have been there naturally with the sun's current position.

A voice came from the darkness, and someone wearing a large black cloak that covered their face leaned forward. The shadows clung to his features as he walked into the light.

"What do you see?" the figure asked, this time loud enough that Myrddin registered that he was being talked to.

Myrddin pointed at the cauldron with his wand. "Nothing we haven't seen for an eon. In other words, nothing new."

"Then why are you still looking? Show me. Show me what you see."

Myrddin waved his wand above the cauldron and the water changed color once more. A red streak flashed across the water's surface: a meteor. The piece of space rock flew toward the earth. It was obvious what would happen upon impact.

The hooded figure sighed as he pulled away. "This is sooner than I assumed it would be. We need to assemble the Riders."

Myrddin was still staring at the cauldron. "They aren't ready yet," he whispered. "*She* is not ready yet."

"She?"

Myrddin nodded. "The one we've been waiting for. She is female. A youth. And a human."

The figure hissed. "A girl, *and* a human? We haven't had a female Rider for centuries. And we've *never* had a human Rider."

Myrddin touched the cauldron's surface. The liquid bubbled under the old wizard's fingertips, and wisps of smoke in the shape of dragons lifted from the surface. "And now you know why I'm hesitant."

"I do," the figure said as he placed his hand over the cauldron's surface. Immediately the liquid calmed and the wisps of smoke formed an image of a girl. "Then get her ready."

"There is one more added complication."

"What is it now?"

"The girl—the human—she's blind."

The figure waved a bony hand. "Hardly important. Do what you have to. Get her to Middang3ard."

The cloaked form walked to the wall and disappeared. Myrddin turned from his cauldron and shook his head as he sat down. Things were moving faster than he'd anticipated. Hopefully their gamble on the Dragonrider program would pay off.

CHAPTER TWO

Alex pulled up the coordinates Jim had sent her and locked them into her HUD's navigation. It wasn't quite autopilot, but it was close enough. The battle wasn't too far away—a ten-minute ride if Alex decided to take her time.

But it seemed like whatever was happening was important enough for Alex to focus on getting there as soon as possible.

She pulled back on the imaginary reins of the dragon and sped up. It still helped her to imagine there were actual reins so she didn't get caught in the disorientation of moving in unison with her dragon.

As she descended from the clouds, the air got thicker and breathing came more easily. From this distance, she could see the skirmish with three other Dragonriders and could tell they were her party members.

One of the perks of being a Dragonrider was that the HUDs automatically upgraded the eyesight of their Riders, not that Alex would have noticed. She did, however, think it was funny that she'd spent her entire life not being able to see, and here in the game, she had better vision than most of the players of *Middang3ard*.

It looked like Jim was the only one of Alex's party who'd shown up for the fight. That was obviously the reason he'd messaged her with such urgency. She was surprised he decided to show up for a fight without the rest of the party.

Alex patched her HUD to Jim's so they could talk. "Hey, Jaws. What are you doing here all by yourself?" she asked. "Didn't feel like waiting for anyone else?"

Jim's voice crackled through the HUD as Alex sped toward him. "Not much of a choice," he replied. "No one else was able to make it today. Not like it matters, though. There's a couple of people from other parties coming on the raid. We'll have more folks backing us up than usual."

As Alex got closer, she could see Jim was totally outnumbered by the swarm of harpies who surrounded him. Initially, she'd thought the mass of wings was a bunch of dragons flying together. Jim was weaving in and out of the swarm, trying to take down as many as he could.

Fun wasn't the word for what Alex was ready for. She dove headfirst into the swarm of harpies. As she pulled back, her dragon roared and spread its wings to catch the warm thermals that allowed it to lift into the air as it shot ether fire from its mouth.

The dragon's fire scorched the closest harpies, and their screams filled the air as they scrambled, grasping at whatever they could rip into.

Alex had fought harpies in the sky before; they weren't difficult enemies. They liked to group around one target. Facing them by yourself could prove to be difficult, but if you had backup, it was a cakewalk.

Jim had been doing well so far. He probably could have cleaned them up without issue, but with Alex's help, this would be over before it even began. *Might as well take the chance for some practice*, Alex thought to herself.

A harpy with a little bit more intelligence than the rest came for Alex, while most of the others tried to attack her dragon.

Alex didn't even issue commands. She knew her dragon would snatch up any harpies close by and tear them to bits by instinct. The only thing Alex had to focus on was the harpies that knew enough to go for the Rider.

As one swooped down, Alex felt a surge of excitement. She'd seen some of the veteran Dragonriders try something like this, and she'd always wanted to give it a shot. This was a simple enough encounter that she could.

She imagined herself letting go of her reins to allow the dragon more freedom of movement. Then, as the harpy descended, she pulled out her bō staff, an elegantly-crafted piece she picked up from the corpse of a dead monk. It was the first weapon she'd found, and her favorite.

Veteran players had mocked her for holding onto her first weapon, but over the last few months, they'd been silenced by her proficiency.

Alex vaulted off her dragon into the air and felt the weightlessness that had originally terrified her. Her dragon darted forward and attacked the nearest harpies.

Alex sailed through the air with her bō tucked behind her back. She snapped a harpy's neck with a single flick of her wrist, swung herself onto its back, and rode the falling body into the next harpy.

She jumped from the dead harpy to another and wrangled her bō around its neck to steer it to the next. She let her grip relax briefly to bash the head in before settling back on the harpy she rode.

She guided it back and leaped off, casually hitting it between its eyes as she landed on the back of her dragon.

With a yank of the reins, she commanded the dragon to shoot another blast of ether flame.

Jim was faring well as he swooped through the swarm and fired blasts of fire where he aimed his bow. He picked off any harpies who were foolish enough to try to get close to him. Alex absentmindedly admired his work; the boy was an excellent shot.

As Jim lined up his shot, he also activated his dragon's missile launcher and fired a volley of heat-seeking missiles to compliment his rapid shots. Each of his arrows hit its mark.

Within a couple of minutes, Alex and Jim had taken out the harpies. The skies were silent when Jim guided his dragon to Alex. "Nice little fight, right?" he asked.

Alex sat on her ether dragon and yawned theatrically. "I mean, if you call that a fight," she replied.

"I saw that little move you pulled. It was amazing."

"Just trying to keep up with you, Jaws."

He laughed as he brushed his hair out of his face. Alex could see he was blushing. She'd read about people blushing for years. It never ceased to amaze her how red Jim's face could get. "So, what are we up to today?" she asked.

Jim pointed east and cleared his throat. "There's a big raid happening today," he explained. "The rest of the party is meeting us near Mt. Caton. I went ahead to clear the way and introduce us to the other Riders. It's the expansion raid."

Alex felt a twinge of irritation but tried to keep her face from betraying her emotions. "I don't need you to plan my quests for me," she finally replied.

"Wasn't trying to. I wanted to see what the expansion has in store for us, and I didn't want to wait around for you to figure out if you want to do it."

The irritation Alex felt was quickly replaced by embarrassment. She hoped she wasn't blushing. "Oh, all right.

Makes sense, I guess. Well, how about we go meet those other Riders and get this thing going?"

He smiled, and Alex felt her heart skip. "Sounds good. Let's find out what all the fuss is about."

Jim turned east and sped off. Alex chased him until she overtook him, then she took the lead.

CHAPTER THREE

Alex and the Dragonriders arrived at the area the coordinates indicated. It was a massive mountain, and its peak was covered in clouds. It was larger than anything Alex could have imagined.

She'd heard of Mt. Everest and had been given descriptions of different objects she could feel and touch to give her context, but she could never have dreamed of anything this large.

This was the same mountain she always saw in *Middang3ard*. It was visible almost anywhere on the map, and it looked like an unattainable dream. It was easily more than a month's journey by horseback.

Whatever this mission entailed, Myrddin had obviously had a plan if he'd placed the mountain too far for the average player to consider reaching.

Jim was riding beside Alex when he pointed to the mountain and asked, "You see the cave ahead?"

Alex squinted to follow the imaginary line of Jim's finger. She could see the cave, and there was someone standing in it. "That must be Shiva. We need to get into the cave."

Alex didn't waste time waiting for the other Riders to catch on to what she was doing, but Jim and the rest of her party were ready for that. Alex was always the first to dive into battle.

It wasn't as if she were Leroy Jenkins-ing the situation. She wouldn't have gotten the reference anyways; she was just fast. Faster than anyone else. No one ever had to pull her out of trouble. They just had to catch up to her.

As Alex raced toward the mountain cave, she could see Shiva better. The four-armed god wore a belt of human skulls and held a human head in one of his hands. Two of the other hands held scimitars, and the last one a rose.

The blue-skinned god smiled as he held the rose toward Alex. *What the hell did I learn about Shiva?* Alex thought, trying to remember the comparative religion class she'd audited at her local community college.

I wonder if Myrddin based this on any of the stories about Shiva, or if he's using them as a template or something. What should I do, attack?

Alex slowed to a glide. Before she had time to figure out how best to handle the situation, another Dragonrider zoomed past her. "For the realm!" he screamed as his dragon's shoulder-blade blaster fired.

Alex shook her head. She could already tell this was a bad idea. A better idea would be to get out of what was going to quickly become Shiva's warpath. Still, Alex was mildly interested to see what kind of fighter Shiva was, and what kind of god Myrddin had programmed.

Shiva raised his hands. A few laser blasts hit his palms, but most were deflected before they got anywhere near him.

Shiva smiled sweetly as he shook his head at the Rider. "Foolish human," Shiva said, speaking softly. "Do you think I fear the monstrosity of flesh and technology you've created? I was born at the time of the first dragon. I have ended countless cycles of repetition and watched the fireworms make their way to the earth again, a millennium before any Dust Child had reached for its first fruit. You will find me meditating. Farewell."

Shiva's rose stretched and hardened, transforming into a long silver trident. He threw the trident, and it impaled the eye of the attacking Rider's dragon. The dragon screamed in pain and flailed.

The Rider tried to get control, but Shiva thrust one of his swords through the Rider's chest. The Rider's screams mixed with the dragon's as they plummeted toward the ground.

Even though it was a game, it always shocked Alex to see a player die. Myrddin hadn't wasted any expense when it came to death animations. Blood smelled like iron, and the pain on the faces of fellow players was always gruesome.

In a morbid way, it was one of the best parts of the game. Sure, you could respawn later if you weren't one of the hard-core "one-lifers," but avoiding seeing your friends in such a dismal position was a good motivator for teamwork. Immersion was where the fun was found.

Alex guided her dragon away from the mountain. She had a bad feeling about what was coming next. There was no way this quest was going to be this easy. A dozen or more Dragonriders taking on one god in a mountain cave?

Myrddin would have created something better, something that would really test the skill of the Dragonriders. Otherwise, why stage this whole thing in the air?

As Alex raced away from the cave, she looked over her shoulder and could now see where the challenge was going to be. Holes had opened all over the mountain, giving it the look of a giant honeycomb. What was even more terrifying was that the mountain seemed to be breathing. Then the bees showed up—billions and billions of them. Alex could see them emerging from the new holes.

The bees had to be huge if Alex could see them in such detail. She wasn't looking forward to seeing them up close. The bugs of *Middang3ard* were easily a thousand times more disgusting than anything she'd heard described in real life.

Maybe everyone I know has just been really bad at describing bugs? Enough people seem to be grossed out by them. I wouldn't be surprised if they were this bad.

Alex regrouped with the Dragonriders, who had finally caught up. They stared at the swarm of bees as it blocked the light of the sun.

Phillis pulled down her HUD as she received a message. "You can see it from down there," she said. "It's like a total eclipse for the players on the ground."

Alex looked through her own HUD and grinned when she saw the percentage of success: -37%. "Perfect," she whispered before flipping her HUD up and turning to the rest of the Riders. "All right, you guys ready to do some real flying?" she shouted. "Jim, you're on me!"

One of the other Dragonriders scoffed as he folded his arms. "Who made you leader?" he asked. "Last time I checked, we were different parties. I don't know how your party likes to do things, but the Growlers don't take kindly to being ordered around, even if it's coming from Boundless."

"I'm not giving orders. You came here to fly, didn't you? I just want to see if you actually can."

The rest of the Riders laughed and followed Alex as she took off toward the swarm of bees.

A bee nearly a third the size of the dragon she rode came for her. It was obvious to Alex that alone, one bee wasn't going to be a problem. The problem arose from the sheer number of them.

Shiva's cave was already obscured by the bees, and there was no way the Dragonriders could kill them all. There were billions, and it didn't look like the mountain was done producing them.

The bee coming for Alex sped above her head as she ducked, pulled her dragon into a turn, and signaled for a stream of ether fire. The fire singed the bee's wings, and it dropped.

That was good. The bees were weak, which meant she could fight her way through the swarm into the cavern. That was the clearest strategy she saw.

Jim was now at her side. He usually played as a tank for Alex, but both of them knew the truth: Jim was tanking for the rest of the team. Alex was generally too fast to be tanked for.

Neither Alex nor Jim felt the need to pat each other on the back for their teamwork. They both filled their roles, and things always worked out. This time, though, Jim seemed adamant about staying near her.

"Do you know where the cave opening is?" Jim shouted over the wind.

Alex pointed at the swarm that was quickly approaching. "All I know is that it's past them."

The rest of the Dragonriders had caught up and were whooping and yelling, trying to prime themselves for the fight that was about to happen. Alex never bothered with any of that stuff. It seemed like a lot of bravado for the sake of putting on a show.

A couple of times, Alex had mentioned it snidely to Jim and he'd agreed, but it didn't stop him from shouting along with the rest of the Riders as they raced toward the swarm.

As the first wave of bees turned their attention to the Riders, Alex fell back to let the other Riders go ahead. She wanted to get a better idea about how the bees were going to move. Everything in *Middang3ard* had a pattern, especially the enemies.

It felt callous to think, but not everyone was going to make it out of this raid. That was a simple fact. She might as well learn from their mistakes so they wouldn't become hers.

A Rider on a fire dragon made the first move. His dragon attacked the first wave of bees with its laser blasters, and the bees fell to the earth. It hardly mattered, though, because another wave was right behind and had already overrun them.

The bees were now so close that the blasters couldn't fire. They completely covered the dragon and its Rider and were vibrating together so loudly that Alex could hear them. All at once, they raised their stingers and plunged them into the dragon.

The dragon's scream rang out above the incessant buzzing, and soon the dragon, Rider, and bees were all plunging earthward.

The fight was on. Dragonriders were flying as close as they could to what looked like a giant black tornado. They flew back and forth, dipping in and out of the bee swarm as they unleashed a variety of elements.

The air was hot with fire and electricity as the endless number of bees attacked the Riders. Dragons were dying left and right. Not as fast as the bees but, unlike the insects, there were a finite number of Riders and dragons.

Alex and her party hung back from the battle. They had taken their cue from Alex and were hesitant to join a fight they couldn't win. Alex concerned herself with winning and losing. She knew she was going to win. She just didn't know how yet.

Initially, she had thought flying straight into the middle of the swarm and fighting her way through was the best idea. That strategy had gone out the window the moment she realized how many bees were swarming out of the hive-mountain.

The Rider who had first taunted Alex was doing an amazing job in battle. He was sticking to the outskirts of the swarm, where he and his party picked off bees that made the mistake of getting too close.

When the Rider looked over his shoulder at Alex, he shouted, "I thought you were going to show us how it's done?"

Alex's pride was pricked. At this point, it would be reckless to ride straight into battle, but it didn't keep her from considering doing exactly that. She hoped she wasn't blushing from embarrassment and was glad the jerk teasing her wasn't close by.

Corwyn sighed and leaned against his dragon's neck. "Are we just going to watch the whole fight from the sidelines? If so, I could have skipped the raid instead of wasting my time."

"Going in without a plan doesn't make any sense," Alex explained. "Do you see how many Riders are getting killed?"

"Yeah, I do. At least they're doing something. None of us are one-lifers. We could just respawn and run the raid again. You know, classic MMO style. Run it 'til we break it."

"I don't think Myrddin would have designed something that simple."

"Yeah, the whole swarm of bees coming out of a mountain is *very* original."

Alex kept watching the way the bees moved. There had to be some kind of pattern—and then she saw it.

The bees all flew the same direction—each and every one of them. As they exited the mountain, they flew upward and to the right.

That was what was forming the funnel shape of the tornado. "All right, if you guys want to do something, we might as well," she said. "We start at the top and push our way down."

Jim looked at Alex, obviously puzzled by the idea. "Wait,

so we're just going to do what everyone else is doing?" he asked.

"Yeah, but smarter. Come on."

Alex kicked her dragon into gear and gained height as she flew toward the tornado of bees. If these were anything like the ones in real life, they had a hive mentality. The hive was where they drew their strength, and it was also their weakness.

None of the bees were behaving as individuals, and Alex was going to take advantage of that.

She turned to Jim, who was riding beside her, and said, "I don't need you to tank for me, all right? You need to watch out for everyone else. There are some really good Riders in there who are getting murdered. Try to keep everyone else alive."

Jim nodded and cut his speed a little, dropping back with the rest of the party. "Trust me. I know I'm not taking care of you." He chuckled. "Let's go get that shiny rock."

The party was nearly to the top of the bee funnel. They crested the ornate living structure, and Alex sent her dragon speeding into the swarm.

The bees scattered almost immediately. Alex launched her missiles and unleashed a torrent of ether fire, burning through the insects around her. Just as she predicted, the bees moved in sync, trying to figure out how to maintain their pattern when there was something disrupting it.

That didn't mean the bees weren't attacking, though. Alex swerved in and out of the tornado before popping out of the blackness to get a breath of fresh air and see how far they had descended through the funnel.

If this really is a tornado, it's got to have an eye, Alex thought. She leaned closer to her dragon to be more aerodynamic and dove back into the swirling mass, still following the pattern of the bees while forcing herself into the middle.

Alex's HUD binged. She didn't need to check the message. It was the alert for one of your party members dying. It couldn't have been Jim. Way too soon. Jim would have held out longer than anyone else.

Alex burst into the eye of the bee tornado. As expected, it was completely still, but what she saw in the stillness surprised her.

One bee in the middle was unlike the bees that surrounded it. This bee looked almost human. Its abdomen was extremely long and gaunt and had four wings extending from it. Its remaining two wings were attached to its thorax. A stinger hung bloated from its back end.

The queen bee held her hands up and gestured in what could have only been the pattern of the tornado.

Alex looked to see who had followed her into the eye of the bee storm. Jim popped out of the black cloud of insects and looked around as if he'd emerged from a cave and his eyes needed to adjust to the light. Phillis was right behind him. "All right," Alex said and pointed to the queen bee, "That's what's controlling the other bees."

Jim rushed toward the queen, shouting, "You don't need to say anything else!"

Alex was right behind him, easily matching his speed. Her dragon let out a blast of ether fire as she launched her last two missiles. She was going to have to switch to her blasters after this.

The blasters were faster but didn't pack as much of a punch as her missiles did. *That shouldn't matter too much*, Alex thought. *The missiles should take care of her.*

The missiles connected with the queen, resulting in a massive explosion. Jim and Alex swerved to avoid the blast. The wave hit Phillis, pushing her back but not out of the tornado's eye.

The queen bee was still flying and hardly had a scratch on

her. After a moment, her thousands of eyes focused on the Riders. Then, in a blink, she was in front of Alex. The queen was fast. Her mandibles dripped saliva as she swiped them at Alex.

The Rider ducked, barely avoiding the queen's attack. Then she launched an uppercut that caught the bee in the jaw and pushed her back a little, which was all the room Alex needed. She leaned forward, and her dragon nosedived as fast as it could.

The queen raised her hand and pointed at Phillis. A column of bees shot from the tornado and hit Phillis' dragon, which screamed as it spiraled toward the other side of the insectoid mass.

Alex stopped on a dime and turned before firing her blasters at the column of bees attacking Phillis. "Keep them off of her!" Alex shouted as her dragon let loose another blast of ether fire.

Jim flew toward Phillis and fired at the attackers. Suddenly the queen appeared in front of Jim and slashed at him. From below, Alex fired her blasters at the queen, sending her flying away from Jim. Once she regrouped, the queen sent another column of bees after Jim, but he easily evaded the attack.

Alex looked at the tornado around her and saw that the bees were flying erratically. The integrity of the tornado was broken. "Now!" Alex shouted. "Ignore her! I don't think we can take her. Head for the cave's mouth!"

Alex bolted toward the cave, and Jim and Phillis followed. Flying through the insects was easier now; they hardly noticed the three Riders. The queen must still be too distracted after fighting them one on one to also control her minions.

With that thought, the queen suddenly appeared in front of Alex, who was ready for her and didn't waste her time returning the attack. Instead, she dodged and continued pushing through the insect bodies in front of her.

The cave could be seen through the thick of the bees now. Alex imagined snapping the reins of her dragon, prompting it to increase its speed toward the cave's entrance. There was another beep in her HUD; Phillis must have gotten hit by the queen. Alex was too close to turn around, though. She had to make it to the cave.

She burst through the last of the bees and skidded into the opening. She dismounted her dragon and ran to the back of the cave. When she turned, she saw that Jim was coming toward the cave, and he was smiling. He made it.

That happiness was short-lived. The queen bee appeared in front of Jim and slashed him across the chest before she plunged her stinger into his dragon's head.

Jim screamed in pain as his dragon roared, and they plummeted to the ground. Alex reached out for Jim, but she was too late, and his hand slipped through her grasp.

When the queen turned to face Alex, she didn't attack. Instead, she pointed past Alex to a passageway in the cave.

Alex didn't need to be persuaded to get as far from those bees as possible. Away from the insects and away from the guilt. Even though she knew it wasn't real, she always hated seeing her party members die. It didn't help that she was often the last one left, but she pushed those feelings aside to concentrate on the mission. As long as she finished the raid, her squad would get the experience points.

The mission was what mattered. It was the entire reason they were here.

As Alex inched past her dragon, she noticed that the cavern's entrance narrowed the farther you went. That meant Alex wasn't going to be able to bring her dragon, and the idea put her on edge.

Whatever lay ahead was going to test things Alex wasn't

prepared for. She'd assumed the trial was going to depend on her prowess as a Rider.

I guess that part's over. Why the hell would I have to finish a quest that isn't about me riding? she thought.

The hope that the rumors were true flashed in Alex's heart, as bright as the sun. What if it was more than a rumor? What if Myrddin was testing the players to see which ones had the right stuff to go to Middang3ard? If Middang3ard was even real, which she still wasn't sure about.

Anybody could get good at a game. What if this was something else?

Alex pushed the hope and excitement down. Those thoughts wouldn't get her anywhere. She needed to be ready for whatever came at her.

Before she left to go down the tunnel, she kissed her dragon on the snout. Even if the dragon wasn't real, it was a small comfort. They were in this together, whether or not Alex was going to walk down the dark tunnel by herself.

Facing the darkness, she considered her bō before pulling a sword from her inventory. She figured she would need something with an edge, and the sword was magically enhanced. Then, with a sigh, she stepped into the tunnel.

The farther she walked, the tighter the space got, until she felt like she was going to be smothered by the walls. However, in the distance, there was a light. *Guess this time I am supposed to go toward the light,* she joked to herself.

The tunnel broadened as Alex drew closer to the illumination. She stood in front of a door that led into what appeared to be a large golden room, but really, the room was more than golden. Every inch of the room was covered in gold leaf. There was a gold table covered in candles that cast a golden light across the space. The floor was littered with various gold weapons: ornately-crafted swords and axes, and bows with peacock feather-fletched arrows.

Golden statues of Shiva, all holding swords, filled the cavern as well. The cavern walls were covered in golden portraits of gods and beings Alex had never seen before but somehow knew were divine.

In the middle of the room sat Shiva. His back was facing Alex, and the god did not bother to rise when she entered the room. "It looks as if you are the only one to survive," he said softly.

Alex's curiosity was piqued by Shiva's calm. "What do you mean, the only one?" she asked.

"All the other Dragonriders failed the quest. You are the only one who remains to finish it."

Shiva rose and turned to face Alex, holding a sword in each of his four hands. "Have the trials of the Jewel of Qa brought me a warrior?" Shiva asked.

Alex waited for the god to attack, but Shiva did not move. He merely held his swords and waited. *Fine. I'll bring the fight to him,* Alex thought.

Alex rushed forward with her sword raised. She swung at Shiva, who easily deflected but didn't return the attack. Alex jumped back and swung her sword once more. The god merely blocked Alex's strike and then stepped forward as if the two of them were engaged in some kind of dance.

Shiva posed with his swords, looking like something that had walked out of Alex's textbook on comparative religions.

"Is that all *Middang3ard* has taught you?" Shiva asked. "The ways of a warrior?"

Alex took another step back. She should have known better than to think she could fight the incarnation of life and death. She'd been expecting a hard fight, but this was pointless. What else was she missing?

Shiva still wasn't attacking. He stood there with a bemused smile on his face. *That isn't the face of someone trying to kill me,* Alex thought, *so why the hell am I trying to kill him?*

Alex tossed her sword on the ground, then took a deep breath and went to one knee in front of Shiva.

As Alex knelt, the golden statues of Shiva sprang to life and surrounded Alex. Their swords rose as they stared down at the girl.

Alex had to use all of her restraint not to grab her sword as Shiva started to laugh. "Did the trials also bring me a fool?" Shiva asked.

None of the statues moved after their initial aggression. Alex watched them out of the corners of her eyes. If the statues did attack, she would easily be able to evade and get back to her dragon, but the statues were just as unmoving as they had been before. *Here goes nothing,* Alex thought.

Alex cleared her throat as she raised her right hand, made a fist, and pressed it to her heart. "Lord Shiva, I declare my loyalty to you," she pledged. "Since you are a guardian of Middang3ard and the protector of the Jewel of Qa, I apologize for my brashness earlier."

Shiva smiled, and the golden guards surrounding Alex collapsed into heaps of gold dust. "You will serve me?" Shiva asked as he approached Alex, dropping his swords on the way.

"I serve Middang3ard, and since you are a guardian of the realm, I serve you as well."

Shiva raised two of his hands and cupped the other two in front of his chest as if they were holding something. The Jewel of Qa shimmered into a palm. "As is customary for the gods of Middang3ard, allow me to present you with a gift to honor our allegiance," Shiva stated.

Alex rose and reached for the jewel. As soon as her hand touched the cold surface, the world went black.

CHAPTER FOUR

Alex felt at home, and the thought disturbed her. She could still perceive the world around her, including the wind on her skin and the heat of the room. There was no doubt in her mind that she was still in *Middang3ard*, even if the world had gone black.

It was like someone had turned off the lights. Absent-mindedly, she wondered if other players would have been freaking out by now.

Being in the dark was nothing new for Alex.

A voice broke Alex's concentration. It was soft and frail— an ancient voice, one that had spoken many languages during its years.

Alex didn't know how she knew any of this, but she felt it deep in her bones. Whoever was speaking had been alive for a very long time.

The voice said, "Please, don't be alarmed. I wanted to speak with you in person to congratulate you on your achievement. Not many have passed this final judgment. You're among the elite in your class."

Alex turned, or at least she thought she did. The spatial

awareness and tactile perceptions she'd had a moment earlier had vanished.

Now it felt like she was floating in a large bowl of water. It was as if gravity had been sucked out of the room. She couldn't locate the source of the voice, no matter how hard she tried. "Who are you?" she finally asked. "Are we still in the game?"

Directly in front of Alex, the air seemed to shimmer and tear open as if reality was being ripped apart. After a moment, a silver and gold portal appeared before her. Her vision returned, and as she peered into the portal, she saw an entirely different world than the one she'd come from. It was just a slice, but she recognized enough to know it wasn't *Middang3ard*. The sliver was of a room, and it reminded her of her grandfather's study. The furniture was vaguely mid-century Victorian.

Out of the portal stepped Myrddin. He wore a well-pressed gray suit and a bowler hat. In one hand, he held the Jewel of Qa, and in the other, a cane on which he leaned as he walked toward Alex.

She instinctively backed away.

Myrddin tossed the jewel into the air and it vanished. He then extended his hand to Alex and smiled sweetly. "I am Myrddin, the CEO and creator of *Middang3ard*." He waited for Alex to shake his hand.

Slowly, she became aware of having a body again. She looked down at her hand as she extended it toward Myrddin. "*The* Myrddin?" Alex asked.

"The one and only."

Alex was speechless. There was so much she wanted to tell him. She wanted to thank him for his gift of *Middang3ard*, and to explain how playing this game had completely changed her life. She wanted him to know that who she was in his game was someone she could never dream of being in real life, and that the game often felt more real than her life did.

But there was too much to express. Instead, she stared silently at the old man.

Myrddin chuckled. "I was expecting you to be a little more talkative," he admitted. "You spend so much time bantering with your fellow players."

Alex cleared her throat and scratched the back of her head nervously. "Uh, it's a surprise, is all. I wasn't expecting any of this. And I wasn't expecting to see you either. It's just...a lot to take in."

"What were you expecting to happen?"

"I don't know. I don't think I was truly expecting to be the only one to make it to the jewel."

"You were not only the only one today to finish the raid, but also the only human to have completed the trial."

Alex's eyes narrowed. Did he just say, "the only human?"

Myrddin continued speaking as if he hadn't noticed Alex's surprise. "I personally didn't think any humans were going to pass the final—"

"Wait, you mean, like, other players playing as other races, right?"

Myrddin's eyes twinkled as he waved his hand. Two chairs and a coffee table appeared in the blackness of the room. The chairs were fluffy, homey things you might find in a professor's office.

Two cups of coffee sat on the table, along with a variety of cookies. "No, I do not mean humans pretending to be elves or dwarves," Myrddin said as he took a seat at the table. "I meant what I said—that you were the only human who managed to complete the trial."

Alex took a seat; she had to. It felt like the rug had been pulled out from under her. Different races? Did that mean...

Myrddin took one of the cups of coffee and sipped it as

he reclined in his chair. "I've been looking forward to meeting you for some time," he explained. "You're one of our top Dragonriders. The best human Rider by a large margin."

Alex turned to face Myrddin, her heart continuing to race. "You said there were other races. You mean, people who aren't human? Like, elves? Real elves?"

"I'm assuming you've heard the rumors by now."

"That Middang3ard is real. That this isn't just a game. That there's a real place all of this is based on and you're asking people to go there."

"Do you believe them?"

Alex remained quiet. She knew deep down she'd always believed Middang3ard was a real place. It had to be. There was no way anyone, no matter how large the creative team, could have dreamed up such a fully fleshed-out world.

That being said, Alex didn't usually let her imagination run away with her. Maybe she just hadn't experienced enough videogames to have seen past the magic.

Regardless, Middang3ard was probably just an island someplace that the elite gamers were being treated to. There was no way an entirely different world could exist.

Alex sadly shook her head. It almost hurt her to say out loud that she didn't believe Middang3ard was a place she could go. More than anything else, what hurt was realizing that even if Middang3ard was real, it was not a place she could experience.

Blind in real life meant blind in real life. "No," Alex whispered. "I don't believe in Middang3ard."

Myrddin hadn't stopped smiling. He placed his cup of coffee on the table. "You believe what you can see, don't you?" he asked.

Alex gave Myrddin a look of incredulity. Did he know about her eyesight? His statements had become increasingly pointed on the topic of sight. Was he teasing her?

Myrddin raised his hand and a spindly oak wand appeared between his fingers. He waved it, and the world around them exploded in color. It was as if they were being pulled through the universe at a speed Alex couldn't comprehend.

But this was virtual reality. Nothing Myrddin showed her was going to change her mind. *So why is he trying so hard?* she wondered. What would Myrddin gain by deceiving her?

When the colors finally settled into patterns that were more manageable, Alex found herself sitting in a cottage. A look around revealed it was a study much like she would have imagined Myrddin would have if he was an old wizard living in the shire.

The study was filled with bookcases stuffed with ancient-looking scrolls and tomes. There was a sofa that looked like it had been around since the dawn of time. A bearskin rug covered the floor, but it wasn't a bear like anything Alex had ever read about before.

During her time in *Middang3ard*, she'd taken every chance to read anything with pictures. She'd seen what a bear looked like. This was something close but off. Two great antlers stretched from the bear's head and its feet were webbed.

Myrddin and Alex were still sitting at the same table. They must have been in his study the entire time. "This is still just virtual reality, though," Alex said. "I haven't taken my headset off yet."

Myrddin rose from his chair and headed toward the door. "Are you coming?" he asked as he looked over his shoulder.

Alex stood and walked after Myrddin. There wasn't anything else to do.

The two of them walked through a living room that wasn't much different from the study. There was a welcoming fireplace, but the predominant theme of the living room was the same: books and scrolls.

The biggest difference was that the living room was a mess. There was hardly anywhere to walk; Alex had to step over the books that covered the floor. "Do you live here?" Alex asked.

Myrddin bent over and picked up a book, looked at the title for a few seconds, then placed it on a bookcase as he walked by. "As you said, we are still in virtual reality," he explained. "This is a virtual representation of my home pulled directly from my mind.

"Most of *Middang3ard* is based on my experiences and memories of the real Middang3ard. Some things were fleshed out by other mages and wizards. We never add anything that would not be found in the real place, but there are things we hide. Some of the more fantastical elements would break the average human's ability to suspend disbelief, and we try to avoid that situation. I find it much easier to gauge the audience's participation in my creation when they forget it isn't real."

Myrddin opened the door and stepped outside. Alex followed.

Night, in a way Alex had never experienced night in *Middang3ard*, had descended on the cottage. The air was crisper than she'd ever felt. She could scent flowers she'd never smelled before.

Now that she thought of it, she'd only ever smelled familiar flowers while playing in *Middang3ard*. She'd never run across anything unfamiliar.

Food smelled mostly like her mother's meals. The first time it rained, all of *Middang3ard* had smelled like her favorite park during the first few hours of a fresh downpour.

Myrddin sat down on the grass and sighed softly as he lit a pipe. "Do you notice the difference?" he asked. "Even in this place? Can you sense how it's different?"

Alex didn't want to admit it out loud, but she felt the

difference. If she'd thought the simulation of *Middang3ard* was real, she didn't know where she was right now. This was real in a way she'd never experienced in VR before.

Myrddin pointed into the distance, where a young man was coming over the hill. "This is an undiluted memory," Myrddin explained. "It's created through a combination of tech and magic. The VR program works in a similar way, albeit not as succinctly. Things such as taste or smell are lifted from the player's subconscious, but all of this is coming straight from me. It is undiluted. Pure, you could say."

"It smells different," Alex commented.

"Yes, it does. Like nothing you've ever smelled before, correct?"

"Never. Not in my entire life."

"If you did not believe this last mission was going to bring you to Middang3ard, why did you put forth such an effort to finish it?"

Alex bit her lip as she tried to think of why it had been so important to finish the mission. Her initial distrust of Myrddin was gone.

"I finished because it was my mission," Alex finally said, deciding to be as honest as possible. "If I take a mission, it's my responsibility to my party and myself to finish it, no matter what."

"Why would you care so deeply about something that is just a game?"

"I-I don't know…"

Myrddin let out a cloud of nearly translucent smoke that took the shape of a boat filled with oarsmen rowing in the ocean of the night until they were out of view. "You've never thought *Middang3ard* was just a game. You'll make an excellent Dragonrider."

"I am a Dragonrider."

Myrddin shook his head as he chuckled. "No, you are

not," he said sweetly. "You have learned how to ride a pale simulacrum of a dragon in a video game. You will need to retrain. Riding a true dragon is something entirely different. Hell, you and your dragon might not even get along."

Alex didn't understand Myrddin at first, but then his words settled in as she thought of her relationship with her dragon. There wasn't one. Her dragon and those of other Riders didn't have personalities. "What are real dragons like?" Alex asked.

"You could find out for yourself."

"You mean, go to Middang3ard?"

"We need you."

Alex considered the proposition. She still had no idea why Myrddin wanted her to come to Middang3ard. It was obvious she'd been training for something she was completely unaware of. Was there really something that evil, to cause Myrddin to recruit players through the game?

Alex cleared her throat, having nothing better to do. "I'm sorry. I can't go," Alex whispered.

Myrddin casually continued smoking his pipe. "Why is that?"

"You don't need to—"

"Is it because you're too small? Too young? I assure you, our elvish Riders are nearly as small as—"

"I am not small!"

"If you're afraid of gender discrimination, our facilities are quite—"

"Dude, it's almost 2020. That's the least I'd expect from you."

Myrddin leaned forward as he extinguished his pipe. For the first time, she felt like she could truly see how old he was. It was like looking at a shadow of a human being. He looked as if he were made of paper.

"Whatever it is you think makes you unfit for the true

Middang3ard, I don't care," he argued. "I have gleaned what kind of person you are. You could be our…oh, confound it… uh, our Luke Skywalker."

Alex laughed despite herself. "'Luke Skywalker?' When was the last time you saw a movie?"

Myrddin laughed as well and leaned back in the grass to stare at the stars. "Too old? I don't have much time for the theater. What would be an equivalent example?"

"Kylo Ren is pretty cool."

"Isn't he a villain? Serving the Sith Order?"

"I thought you didn't have time to go to the movies?"

Myrddin sat up as he smiled. "My great-great-grandchildren have been talking about their Halloween costumes incessantly. I've managed to pick up which side is good or bad."

"Well, he is kinda bad, but he's mostly a badass."

"My point is, we need you."

Alex stood up abruptly and looked around at the world Myrddin had crafted from his memories. "I'm sorry. I can't," she blurted before reaching up and imagining herself disconnecting her VR headset. She logged off and left behind everything about *Middang3ard* she loved.

CHAPTER FIVE

A lex lay in her bed in the darkness, a darkness she was familiar with. It was her home. For the first time in her life, she was happy to be back in that home. What Myrddin had said to her was unsettling.

And that was putting it mildly.

Part of what he said seemed too good to be true. Other parts seemed to be outright lies, but that might have just been what she was telling herself. It was easier to say Myrddin was full of it than admit the real Middang3ard was out there, and she was barred from it for reasons outside her control.

After Alex felt she'd done a substantial amount of moping, she leaned over and reached for her phone. She usually charged it directly next to her pillow, but sometimes when she was flustered by her parents, she would forget where she'd placed it.

Luckily, years of repetition were hard to forget, and her phone was right where she normally left it. She hit the home screen and said, "Open *Middang3ard* player messages."

The phone AI assistant answered in a bubbly tone. "Three

new messages. Would you like me to play them for you, Alex?"

"Who are they from?"

"One message is from Jim, and the two messages marked urgent are from Myrddin."

"Play the message from Jim."

Alex got out of bed as she increased the speakerphone's volume. She walked slowly toward her closet, using the tips of her toes to feel around to see if there was anything on the floor, though there rarely was.

Much like the placement of her cellphone, there were habits she'd drilled into her brain a long time ago. Picking up after herself was one of them. There wasn't anything worse than waking up in a rush and stumbling over a book while trying to get dressed.

The only thing Alex ever left on the floor were her slippers. They were made in the likeness of a snarling jackalope and were extremely cozy. Slipping them on was like slipping on a hug. Alex thought it was one of the single most enjoyable aspects of life.

Jim's voicemail started to play. "Hey-yo! Alex, I saw you cleared the level. We kinda figured you did when you didn't respawn with the rest of us. Obviously, congratulations."

Jim paused awkwardly before continuing, "The rest of the guys wanted to know if you would be down to run the raid with us again soon. We figured you probably got a bunch of cool loot, and that might give us an advantage. I think you might be the first Dragonrider to finish the raid."

Alex felt around in her closet for the top she was looking for. It had a rhinestone applique she really liked. Her mom had told her it was a design of something extremely girly like a unicorn or something, but Alex didn't care. She just liked the feel of the tiny stones.

Jim's voice paused. "Also, we were wondering if, you

33

know, the whole invitation was true? Is there really a Middang3ard? Call me when you get a chance. I know you have homeschooling or something lame to do today. Talk to you later."

Alex grabbed a pair of pants and slipped on her sandals before moving to her desk. She picked up her foldable white cane and attached it to her belt loop. *Was it real?* Alex asked herself. *Sure felt pretty real.*

She figured she could tell Jim about the whole situation when she felt like it. She'd have to come up with a reasonable excuse why she'd rejected what could have been the most exciting thing to ever happen to her.

Fear?

Maybe it was that simple.

Fear of failing. Fear of being reminded she was blind. Fear of having something she wanted more than anything in the world dangled in front of her. Not everyone got a chance to be a hero. What if that chance had just passed?

It's not like it even matters, Alex thought. *I can't see. Even if it is real, I can't see any of it.*

For a second, Alex thought about climbing back into bed. Then she smelled breakfast downstairs. Her mom, Liza, was making breakfast with her dad, George. They were frying bacon. Dad must have been cooking because they weren't using the oven.

Alex could smell that the bacon fat was burning, slightly overcooking the bacon. George had made bacon once a few years ago and forgotten he was cooking. He'd walked away and left the bacon to keep frying.

Alex had been told the bacon had burned to the bottom of the pan, and she'd never forgotten that smell. It was like all of the best things left a little too long.

There was also the golden scent of pancakes. Years ago, she wouldn't have known to call the smell golden, but when she started playing *Middang3ard*, she'd realized that was the smell—golden and perfect. Alex couldn't smell syrup, though. She wondered if her parents had pulled it out of the fridge yet.

She walked out of her bedroom and touched the wall, her index finger finding the edges of a photo frame. She tapped the frame lightly before running her hand beneath it and heading toward the staircase. Her head was still a little fuzzy from signing out of VR.

Usually, Alex wouldn't have bothered with all the precautions going downstairs. She'd been walking from her bedroom to the kitchen for almost seventeen years, but since she started playing *Middang3ard*, there were always a few moments of adjusting to not being able to see again.

Going from being able to see in the VR world to back to the darkness in the real world had never really bothered her.

Except for today.

No, it still doesn't matter, she thought. *Nothing has changed, just because I had one conversation with a crazy old man.*

When Alex came to the stairwell, she sat down and leaned against the banister. She could smell better out here. She listened to the sound of her mother tapping eggs with a knife to crack them. It sounded different than when her father cracked his eggs against the side of the pan.

She could also smell the warm scent of the butter heating in the egg pan. Butter never really smelled like butter unless it was in a pan. Otherwise, it smelled like waiting.

George's voice broke Alex's thoughts. "Hey, honey!" he called. "You finally out of bed?"

Alex stood and descended the stairs, resting her hand on the banister and taking each step slower than usual. "Yeah, I'm up, Dad," she yelled back. "Just got out of *Middang3ard* and smelled that you guys were cooking up a feast."

George and Liza laughed. It was definitely one of Alex's

favorite sounds. When her parents laughed in sync, it sounded like love, like something true and unchanging. It was something solid you could reach out and touch and hold close because it was never going to leave.

Alex crossed the living room, unfolding her cane to be safe, and tapped where she knew the furniture was, stepping to the side to avoid various pieces as she walked into the kitchen, where she took a seat. Her world might have been dark, but it was filled with textures she could never take for granted.

Now that she was in the kitchen, she could smell her father's aftershave and her mother's deodorant. Neither of her parents had bothered trying new products since Alex was born. Now, anytime Alex smelt their brands of deodorant and aftershave, she couldn't help but think of her parents.

Liza cleared her throat and asked, "You thirsty? Would our Sleeping Beauty like orange juice?"

Alex reached across the table to see if there was any toast. She thought she'd caught the faint whiff of perfectly toasted bread. Her fingers met something crusty, and she knew she'd been right. "I wasn't asleep that long," Alex countered.

Alex gingerly felt around until her fingers brushed the jar of jam on the table. She grabbed it and took the spoon out as she snagged a couple of pieces of toast.

George chuckled and said, "Uh-huh, and I'm assuming you know it's almost noon. I'm also assuming you weren't up taking care of your homework. You know we have a lot to get through today."

"I told you guys last night I was going to wake up early and play through a raid with my friends. You were given fair warning. I feel like that should absolve me from any teasing from this point forward."

George set the bacon right under Alex's nose, and she

couldn't keep her mouth from watering. She wanted to reach out and take a handful, but she knew it was too hot. She also knew her parents would tease her mercilessly if she let on that she'd stayed in her room to play videogames despite being ravenous. Playing it cool was the best option.

Alex could smell the eggs her mother brought to the table. Then she heard the groans of her parents relaxing into their chairs and the clank of a glass hitting the table. "Is it safe to eat?" Alex asked. "Or am I being rude if I start now?"

George laughed as he tapped Alex's right hand. Alex raised her hand so she could take the plate of eggs George passed to her. She spooned herself what she assumed was a reasonable amount before tapping her mother's hand and passing her the plate of food.

The Bounds family continued in this way until all the dishes included in the meal had been shared. "Since everyone has been served, you can get started," George said.

For the first few minutes of the meal, no one spoke. Apparently, everyone was as hungry as Alex was. She always appreciated that her parents didn't try to make conversation until it felt natural. They could silently enjoy each other's company while she focused on enjoying her meal.

Liza was an amazing cook. For a long time, Alex assumed she'd had this opinion because she loved her mom and was used to her cooking, but as Alex started staying over at friends' houses for the night, she found she was blessed to live with a gourmet chef.

The kitchen was the room Alex felt the most comfortable in. She'd lost track of how many mornings and nights she'd sat at the table listening to her parents cooking and singing together. Occasionally, they convinced Alex to dance with them.

When Alex was ten, they started to teach her how to cook. They'd helped her memorize which fruits and vegetables were which, and instructed her how to smell when something was ripe. When Alex cooked for her friends, everyone made a huge deal out of it.

George's cooking style was not as precise and detailed as Liza's, but there was one area in which he could not be beaten: his abnormal understanding of meat. Chicken, steak, lamb, alligator—it didn't matter. If it was meat, George could make something divine.

Once the initial delight of the meal had faded into normalcy, Liza poured herself another cup of orange juice. Alex heard her mother lean back in her chair. "So, how was your game today?" Liza asked.

Alex wasn't prepared for her mother to ask her about *Middang3ard*. Her parents didn't usually ask her about gaming unless it seemed like it was going to get in the way of her studies. It was a hobby they didn't understand.

Anytime Alex brought it up, her parents would go on long rants about how videogames were different back in their day. You had to have more imagination, they would say. Graphics weren't everything.

Yeah, but could they help you see back then? Alex mused.

From the tones of her parents' voices, Alex had started to suspect they might both have been heavy gamers when they were younger.

The proposition from Myrddin was still fresh in Alex's mind. She hadn't quite processed what she was giving up by avoiding *Middang3ard*, but these were all things her parents weren't going to understand. "It was pretty fun," Alex finally said. "Me and the guys completed this raid we got with the free expansion pack. It was really hard. Most players haven't even finished it yet."

George coughed as he choked on his food. "You know, I was just reading a couple days ago about a bunch of physical therapy places using *Middang3ard* to help their clients with their therapy."

Alex swallowed a bit of crispy bacon as she nodded. "Yeah, that would make sense," she agreed. "I've heard there are a lot of people who play *Middang3ard* for that reason. I met this one girl who was in charge of one of the merchant guilds. She was the fastest rider on horseback I've ever seen. We were messaging after a quest together. She used to ride horses in real life until she had an accident a couple of years ago and wasn't able to walk anymore. She obviously couldn't ride either, but then she found *Middang3ard* and was able to get back on a horse again."

"I imagine there are a lot of people like that in the game. You can kind of be whoever you want to, right?"

"Yeah but I prefer to be myself. It's more fun that way."

Alex's dad ruffled her hair and said, "That's what I like to hear."

Liza's chair scraped the linoleum floor as she pushed it back and stood. "You know, even though I was leery about the whole thing, I have to say I respect Myrddin for making such an accessible game."

There was still a hint of mistrust in Liza's voice when she continued, "For all the things companies have been dumping money into VR for, this one seems like it's been the most helpful for people."

Alex could tell her parents were talking around the pink elephant in the room. She didn't mind. It was obvious what they were trying to say. Both of them had been terrified of the idea of Alex plugging into a virtual world.

Now that Alex's parents were seeing VR wasn't something they had to be afraid of, they were beginning to understand it allowed Alex to experience life in a way she'd never been able to before.

Alex tapped her dad's hand and said, "Bacon, please. And

yeah, it is pretty cool to see people being able to do stuff they couldn't before. Not just people like me, either. There are kids who are super shy in real life and they're practically legends in *Middang3ard*, like Kevin from homeschool group."

George laughed loudly as he slapped his knee. "Kevin? That kid's a legend in *Middang3ard*? Now that's kind of awesome." He chuckled. "I didn't know he could speak, to be honest."

"They call him 'Silver-tongue Kevin.' He's a pirate or merchant. Something like that."

Alex heard her mother take a seat again, and the smell of fresh coffee wafted through the air. Liza asked, "So, what's this I'm hearing on the news that Middang3ard is real? It's just a game, right?"

Alex heard fear in her mother's voice. "Oh, no, nothing like that," Alex explained. "It's just a game. It's just...well, there are rumors that *Middang3ard* is based on a real place, and that you'll get invited to go to the real Middang3ard if you beat the final expansion."

Across the table, George slurped his coffee. "What about you?" he asked. "Do you believe Middang3ard is a real place? That would be kind of fantastic. I've seen videos of what the game looks like. Dragons and elves and all that. You think it might be real?"

Alex decided to level with her parents. There wasn't any reason why she couldn't tell them what she actually believed. They didn't need to hear about Myrddin, though.

Alex took a deep breath. "Well, yeah, I believe it's real," she admitted. "I mean, the world is so beautiful and full of life. I think it would be harder to not believe it's real. How could anyone dream up something like that? You guys have seen the screenshots I've sent you, right?"

Liza blew on her coffee, causing a slight whistle. "Ugh, I can't imagine a world like that." She groaned. "All those monsters everywhere. A place where demons walk around. That would be terrifying. Utterly terrifying."

There was a knock on the front door, and Alex heard her mother rise from her chair. "It is another Jehovah's Witness," she muttered. "I am getting *very* tired of explaining why we are happy with our church, thank you very much."

George chuckled as Alex tried to keep from laughing. "So don't be so nice," he suggested. Then he turned to Alex and whispered, "They're not here to convert her. They're here because every time they knock, she invites them in for cookies."

Alex took a sip of her orange juice and, with a giggle, said, "It's always the cookies, isn't it?"

The two of them shared a laugh, one that was abruptly cut off when Liza's scream rang through the air.

It was a sound of pure terror. George jumped up, his chair flying backward and rattling on the floor. "What the hell?" he shouted as he ran toward the front door.

CHAPTER SIX

Alex rushed from the kitchen to the living room. She nearly tripped over her chair while moving so fast. After regaining her balance, she tried to focus on something other than her mother's frantic screams to keep from freaking out.

Now it wasn't just Alex's mother screaming; George had joined in. Both were shouting unintelligibly. Something horrible must be happening.

What if someone was robbing them, or someone had showed up at their door with a gun? It could have been anything, and for the first time in a long time, Alex was completely terrified by what she could not see.

Without thinking about it, Alex reached for the cane hanging from her belt. She quietly unfolded it as she hugged the wall on the opposite side of the door. She knew she couldn't be seen from here. The wall jutted out, and you had to inch around it to get to the front door.

Alex's mother was shouting, "What is it, George? What the hell *is* this thing?"

George had stopped screaming, but he wasn't making any

sense. At first, he was babbling, trying to find the words to describe something. *What could they possibly be looking at?* Alex wondered.

She'd never heard her father lose his cool like this before. It was rare for him even to raise his voice, but here he was, trapped in the throes of a horror Alex could only imagine.

Neither of her parents had been ready for whatever had been at the door, and Alex knew she wasn't either. The only difference was that she had the element of surprise.

Alex's subconscious was saying, "This isn't *Middang3ard*, and you aren't some kind of hero who can swoop in and save the day. You're a blind girl with a walking cane. What can you do to help?"

Not stand here like an idiot, Alex thought. Then she inched around the wall and listened closely to see if she could pinpoint where the threat was.

It was hard to hear over her mother's continued scream-ing. By now, her father had stopped stumbling over his words and was speaking very quietly to whoever was at the door.

Alex jumped out from behind the wall with her walking stick raised. From Liza's and George's voices, she could tell roughly where they were. Whatever was freaking them out was most likely between the two adults.

Alex raced forward like all the times in *Middang3ard*. Even with this being real life, it still felt natural. She'd fought countless gnomes, dwarves, elves, and humans. This wasn't going to be any different.

Alex leapt, her cane poised for an attack, and brought it down on what she hoped was the head of whoever was trying to break into her house. The first thing she noticed was that whatever she hit was soft and spongy. It was not the skull of a person.

It wasn't textured like anything that should show up at

your front door in the middle of the day. The closest thing she could think of was a pillow that had been stuffed with meat.

When she fell back, Liza crouched next to her. Her mother wrapped her arms around Alex's middle, and they both backed away.

George picked up Alex's cane, or at least that was what she figured was happening from the sound of the cane scraping the floor, and shouted, "You need to get the hell out of here right now! We don't want any trouble. You need to leave!"

The sound of the cane swishing back and forth let Alex know George was swinging madly at whatever she'd hit.

As Liza pulled Alex back into the living room, she shouted, "We'll call the cops! I don't have any idea what the hell you are, but the cops will deal with you if you don't leave right now."

The voice that came back was very deep, and almost relaxing. Alex could hear the fear and frustration in the speaker's tone. "I apologize. I apologize," the speaker said. "I was told you'd be expecting me. I am so sorry for the inconvenience."

"How could we ever be expecting anything like you?"

Alex leaned close to her mom and whispered in her ear, "Mom, what's going on?"

Liza replied, "It's a monster. Oh, God, it's horrible. It's the most disgusting thing I've ever seen."

"What kind of monster?"

"What do you mean, what kind of monster? It's a *monster* monster."

Alex could still hear her father swiping at the creature at the front door. "I swear to God, I'll smash your head in if you take one step into my house," George shouted.

The monster stumbled over his words as if he were trying

to find the right thing to say. "I'm so, so sorry. I can come back at a better time if you'd like. I didn't mean to interrupt whatever humans do this early in the morning."

Alex grabbed Liza and pulled her closer. "Mom, tell me what it looks like," she demanded, unable to believe there was a real monster at her front door. *How could this happen?*

Liza took a deep breath as she tried to calm down. "Oh, it's disgusting," she muttered. "It's like a giant, floating, misshapen head, and it has an eye in the middle, with a mouth and fangs. There are these tendrils, and all the tendrils have eyes that keep staring and staring. George, get the gun!"

The creature yelped loudly. *Not the kind of yelp that comes from something that's here to kill you,* Alex thought. "Wait, wait, there's no reason to get firearms involved," the voice said. "Most incidents of gun violence take place in the home. We don't want to contribute to that. Ahh, Myrddin sent me for Alex."

George swiped again at whatever was at the front door. "You stay away from my daughter!" Turning to Liza, he yelled, "Honey, get the shotgun! Go, fast!"

"Wait!" Alex shouted. "Just hold on. I think I know what this thing is."

No one spoke. Only the rapid breathing of everyone waiting to see what was going to happen could be heard. "Myrddin sent you?"

The creature, at least that's what Alex assumed it was, spoke in a perfectly normal human voice. "Yes. I'm here to recruit you."

"Wait, you're a recruiter? Like in the game?"

"Yes."

"You're a Beholder, aren't you?" Alex finally asked.

The creature laughed nervously before saying, "Yes, yes, I am. My name is Manny. I'm here on behalf of Myrddin. I wasn't expecting this kind of greeting, and I must say, I'm a bit flustered. I had heard humans were much more hospitable than orcs, but…"

"Alex," George asked, his voice weary and wavering, "you know what this is?"

"Yeah," Alex nodded. "A Beholder. Basically, it's a floating basketball with a hundred or so eyes jutting out of it."

"How did you—" Liza started.

"I've seen one before."

"Seen?" George muttered.

"Yeah, Dad. In the game. Beholders are the, ah…recruiters in the VR game, and I've seen one before. When I first joined the Riders." She turned her attention to Manny. "What are you doing here?"

"You are Alex the Boundless, the blind Dragonrider, right?"

Alex felt her face go red. If she'd been in *Middang3ard*, she would have hit Manny for saying something like that. She couldn't stand it when people labeled her as blind, but then again, she did it to herself all the time.

Ahh, it was all so frustrating!

It wasn't that she was ashamed of it or anything; it just irked her when people who knew nothing about her reduced her to a single character trait. "My name is Alex," she spat. "And I am a Dragonrider. How did you know I was blind?"

"Myrddin informed before he sent me here."

So, Myrddin did know I'm blind. And he still wants me to come to Middang3ard? she wondered.

Manny cleared his throat. When he spoke again, his voice was closer. Alex assumed he'd floated farther into the house. Neither of her parents seemed to have an immediate issue with it.

"Myrddin asked me to give you a gift," Manny explained. "It seems some of the finer details of coming to Middang3ard may have been left unexplained. Myrddin is, unsurprisingly, not the best at talking to people. Personally, I wish he would just allow me to take care of introductions and recruiting."

Liza snorted derisively. "You, in charge of introductions? You're horrifying!" she exclaimed. Then she caught herself. "No offense."

"I'm going to assume you're only being this rude because you've never seen a Beholder and have no idea of our standards of beauty or attractiveness are, but that is neither here nor there. Alex," Manny said, turning to the young Rider, "would you be so kind as to close your eyes?"

The day had already been weird enough, so Alex didn't see the harm in playing along with what Manny or Myrddin was planning. She shut her eyes tightly.

There was a warm tingling against the back of Alex's head and in her eyelids. Abruptly, the tingling became extremely hot and brought tears to her eyes. She yelped softly before rubbing her closed lids.

When she opened her eyes, she saw the outline of her hands.

She screamed and jumped backward, then whirled around with her eyes wide open, seeing everything for the first time. The world around her was dull gray and green, similar to the color scheme she'd seen in *Middang3ard* before its first big patch. If it wasn't for the game, she wouldn't know what colors were. The game had shown her so much.

Just like now. Except now wasn't a game. It was real life.

For the first time ever, she looked around her house and saw the walls and furniture and the paintings and photographs on the wall. She turned to her parents.

George's face looked uncertain as he gazed at Alex. She turned to face Liza, who was still holding her tightly. She looked at her mother's face and saw the wrinkles and lines and the nose she'd drawn in the palm of her hands as a child.

Alex saw her mother for the first time with her own eyes and cried, "What's happening?"

"It's like Myrddin said. Being blind isn't a problem in Middang3ard, not when there's magic," Manny explained—not that Alex heard him.

She was too busy looking at her parents for the first time. Her parent's faces were…well, beautiful.

Manny seemed to understand the gravity of the moment and awkwardly floated back and forth as if he were pacing. "Maybe, I should give you guys some time alone," he suggested before floating past the family into the kitchen.

Alex was in her room, lying in bed, staring at her ceiling. Staring. She'd read in books for years about people staring—just looking ahead with nothing on their mind, zoning in and out as thoughts bounced around.

She hadn't realized she'd had no idea what staring was like. Letting her mind wander in the blackness she'd grown up in was so much different than this. She couldn't understand how anyone could look at a wall for longer than two or three minutes. There was so much else to see.

After Manny granted Alex her eyesight through some kind of magic, she'd cried for what felt like hours before she realized this was far too big of an occurrence to deal with surrounded by three other people, one of them being a Beholder who was likely from an alternate dimension.

She sat up and looked around her room. It was odd how much she'd decorated without seeing any part of it. She'd chosen the color of the walls based on her parent's descriptions and covered them with posters she'd urged her parents to buy her. The posters were of bands she loved, movies she'd watched with her folks that were particularly important, and other things of that sort. It amazed her how her room could have so much personality, so much of *her* personality, without her ever seeing it.

Out of curiosity, she stood up and went to her bathroom. She flipped on the lights and looked at her favorite shirt, the one she was wearing that was covered in rhinestones. She couldn't help but laugh. Her mother was right; the shirt was gaudy and somewhat disgusting. The drawing of the unicorn looked like something a six-year-old would wear. She was thankful her mother always talked her out of wearing it in public.

Myrddin gave this to me, but is it only so I can go to Middang-g3ard? Alex thought. That seemed extremely cruel to her. What if, after all this, she decided she didn't want to go? Would Myrddin take back her eyesight? What kind of man would do something like that?

The questions were pointless, though. Alex now knew Middang3ard was real beyond a shadow of a doubt. The only thing that mattered at this point was getting there. What did Myrddin have lined up for his recruits on the planet? Were things as dire as the online rumors said?

Folks who had allegedly signed up for Middang3ard were saying there was a huge war going on, one they were hiding from the citizens of Earth. The war was something that could tear apart everything humans knew and loved.

Even with thoughts of war, Alex didn't want to spend the rest of her day in her room when there was so much more to look at. What surprised her the most wasn't that she wanted to explore her neighborhood, it was that she didn't.

There was only one place Alex truly wanted to see, and she needed to talk to Manny about that.

CHAPTER SEVEN

George, Liza, and Manny were in the living room when Alex descended the stairs. Her parents were trying to make small talk with the Beholder.

Even though Alex hadn't had much experience reading her parent's body language, she could tell it was an awkward conversation. Manny kept wiping his face with his eye-tipped tentacles. Occasionally, as he swiped one across his face, Alex's vision would blur.

She walked into the living room and sat between her parents, wedging herself in until they had to move. Manny was floating back and forth, looking as nervous as someone applying for their first job.

He cleared his throat multiple times but didn't say anything. Neither did Alex's parents. It was obvious she was going to be the one to get this conversation going. "How did you do that, Manny?" she asked. "How did you make it so I can see?"

His body puffed up as he smiled brightly, his fangs glimmering. "Well, it's not the real deal," he explained. "I cast a simple spell that allowed you to see through my eyes, so everything wasn't as confusing."

"So, you're saying I can't really see? But you weren't in my room with me. How could I see any of that?"

"Oh, well, I *am* a Beholder," he lectured. "You know, one of the ancients who sees many things. My eyes aren't limited in the human sense. I see everything in this house at once. Each eye sees a different layer of reality. I just tapped you into one."

Alex's heart dropped. Myrddin granting her sight for the sake of helping her *was* too good to be true. She knew she shouldn't have assumed anything else. So, was Myrddin hanging potential sight over her head like a carrot to get her to come to Middang3ard?

George crossed his arms as he leaned forward on the couch. "What is all this about? Does your boss make it a habit to send you to people's houses to scare the crap out of them, or is this a special occasion?"

Most of the Beholder's eyes flipped around to look at George. "I don't think it's intended to scare the crap out of anyone, but it happens often enough," Manny admitted. "Usually, I only meet with the potential recruit, but this was a special situation, with Alex being a minor."

Anger overwhelmed Alex, and she blurted, "I can make my own decisions!"

Liza rested her hand on Alex's and smiled sweetly at her daughter. "Honey, I don't think this is the time to be having the independent teenager conversation."

Liza turned to Manny and asked, "Just what is this recruitment that you and this Myrddin... Did I say that right? What is it that you are trying to recruit my only daughter, who I love enough to kill for, to do?"

Manny forced a smile as he tried to disguise how awkward he felt. "Myrddin wanted to speak with the three of you himself," Manny stumbled. "So, if you don't mind, I can patch him in, and he can explain all this. How's that sound?"

Liza, George, and Alex were silent. All had their arms folded and wore identical annoyed looks on their faces. "Damn, this is a hard crowd," Manny mumbled. "All right, so, let me go ahead and pull Myrddin in."

One of Manny's eyes began to twitch, and the tentacle it was attached to grew longer until it was right in front of Alex's family. The eye jiggled in its socket and went white, then a bright beam shot out from the eye, and a column of light sprang up.

The column slowly took Myrddin's shape.

The old wizard smiled encouragingly at Alex and her parents. "Thank you so much for inviting me into your home," Myrddin gushed. "I have been waiting to finally meet the parents of one of my top players. Your daughter has excelled in *Middang3ard* in a way I never believed a human player could."

George couldn't help but look proud of his daughter— and then Myrddin's words made sense. "Thank you, but, er...did you say *human* players?" he asked. "Implying there are non-human players?"

Myrddin nodded as he took a seat in one of the empty chairs in the room. "Yes, yes." He spoke as if he wanted to rush through the conversation. "We use the *Middang3ard* for basic training for most of the elves and dwarves."

Myrddin fidgeted in his chair before continuing, "Humans are the only race where we use it for recruitment. The rest of the races haven't lost touch with the magical world around them, so they don't need as much convincing."

Despite herself, Liza was interested and leaned forward. "What do you mean?"

Myrddin waved his hand as he spoke. "For them, it's mostly the game of politics, trying to figure out how many recruits we can expect to have and what their nations want as payment—all that diplomatic nonsense. Luckily, the human leaders have been much more accommodating."

"And humans are different?"

"Generally, we only have to deal with the lack of belief on a personal level, and if I'm honest, that is much easier than trying to persuade a Drow lord to promise at least two hundred of his finest warriors instead of enrolling them into his guard. I have *really* lost interest in that conversation."

Liza and George stared at Myrddin blankly. "I'm afraid I'm not following any of this," Liza stated.

Myrddin lowered his head and rested it on his hands. "I'm so sorry. Let me back up some to give you a better idea of what is going on. The world you know is only a fraction of what exists. There are seven realms, or perhaps nine, depending on how you're counting. Those realms are all sandwiched on top of each other."

George scoffed as he sat up in his chair. "You really expect us to believe that load of crap?"

Myrddin gestured toward Manny, who was now rubbing some of his slimy eye tentacles on the fireplace. "My emissary is proof enough of the reality. I heard one of you managed to hit him?"

Alex meekly raised her hand. "It was me," she admitted.

"Fantastic! Even out of the game, you show your warrior spirit. Now that we've covered all that, what do you say about coming to join us on Middang3ard?"

Liza stood up, waving her hands in front of her as if she could wave away Myrddin's words. "Hold on a second," she said. "You haven't told us anything about what you are trying to recruit my daughter for. All you've said is that magic and elves exist."

Myrddin pressed his hand to his chest. "Oh, dear, I am terribly sorry," he apologized. "I neglected the most important thing. These realms are in danger. There is a great evil that threatens the very reality of each and every realm. I believed I had more time to prepare for this evil..."

Myrddin waved his hand and the living room disappeared. They were all now sitting on a ridge. "I was wrong, though," Myrddin whispered.

Off in the distance, orcs were gathering. They were nearly seven feet tall. Their gray bodies were covered in war paint, and all carried axes or swords. "The Dark One came," Myrddin explained. "And with his arrival, he brought death and destruction to the realms."

The orcs in the canyon roared with rage. They clanked their swords and axes on their shields as they gnashed their teeth. Furious, they raced toward Alex and her parents, shredding everything in front of them.

Myrddin walked away from the rest of the group. He held up his wand, and a bright light shone from it. "In all of this, humans have only one group that stands for us: our military. But there is a cross-species group known as the MERCs, and within MERC, we have multiple smaller outfits.

Myrddin paused. "George, your daughter was unknowingly training for one of our most prestigious groups, those known as 'the Dragonriders.' No human yet has been capable of what she has done."

The canyon faded, and Alex was back in her living room sitting between her parents. Myrddin and Manny were still there as well. It became painfully obvious now that none of this was fiction. There was a war going on.

Myrddin shifted in his seat. He didn't look uncomfortable and his stoic face didn't reveal any awkwardness, yet his body would not stop moving. His eyes locked with Alex's and did not blink until Liza spoke up. "Are you saying you want our daughter to go to war?"

Manny glanced around the room, his eyes wild as he tried

to determine where he was supposed to look. "We are at war already," Manny explained. "None of us chose this war. We are already in it."

Liza stood and ran her hands through her hair as tears formed in her eyes. "No, you can't ask this of her. She's only a child. You can't take a child to war. You can't!"

George stood and took Liza in his arms. "Honey, hold on. We need to think about this. We can't jump to any conclusions."

Liza pushed George away, her eyes fierce. "Are you kidding me?" she shouted. "You have to be joking. You're actually entertaining the idea of sending our daughter to war? She isn't even an adult yet, and you want to send her to fight? She could die, George."

George sat back down on the couch and looked at Alex. "If there is a war, who are we to stop her from doing what she thinks is right?"

"Just because you served and think it was the best decision of your life, it doesn't mean everyone else does. Do you remember how worried your parents were? How much sleep we all lost, wondering if you were safe?"

"It doesn't matter," Alex interrupted. "I couldn't go to Middang3ard even if I wanted to. All Manny's done is let me see through his eyes. I'm still blind. Nothing is going to change that. I couldn't ride. Period."

Myrddin looked at Alex and smiled. "Goodness, child, do you think I'm a second-rate sorcerer? Your lack of sight has never been an issue. I can solve this issue with a wave of my hand?"

"But it'll only be solved if I come to Middang3ard?"

Myrddin turned his eyes away from Alex. He took a long time answering. "My services are for those who defend our realm," he finally said. "What I can give you is for Middang3ard and Middang3ard alone, but I am not here to bribe or blackmail you. We need warriors—willing warriors. That is why I have decided that whatever you chose, I will restore your eyesight. Stay and hide, and you will do so sighted. Come and fight, and the same awaits you."

Liza ran over to Myrddin and got in his face. "There is nothing wrong with my daughter," she shouted. "She doesn't need your magic to *fix* her. She's not going. You're not putting her in that kind of danger."

Alex watched her mother speak. Her mom was right. She didn't need to be fixed, but it made her angry that her mom thought she had to speak for her. *I'm not a kid,* Alex thought. *I should at least have a say in all of this.*

Alex opened her mouth to speak, but her mother raised her hand, cutting Alex off before she could say a word. "That's final, young lady," Liza growled. "You're not going to Middang3ard."

CHAPTER EIGHT

George and Liza argued back and forth, but Alex didn't hear anything. She was still in shock from her mother's last words. *She wasn't going to Middang3ard.* Hearing the words spoken aloud was almost too much for her, especially since the decision didn't seem to be hers to make.

Listening and seeing Myrddin describe the state Middang3ard was in against the Dark One had done a little to change her opinion about going, and it didn't help that Myrddin said he would restore her eyesight no matter what she chose. If only the condition had been set that she must come to Middang3ard as well.

At first, it had seemed like a cruel ploy to get her to join his military by preying on her desire to see.

And if he could help her, he could help everyone, right? The more she thought about it, though, the more sense it made. Maybe he *could* help everyone, but as powerful as he was, he was still only one man.

Myrddin couldn't go around curing every disability in the world.

However, it seemed like a moot point at the moment. The

decision had been made. Sighted or not, Alex was staying on Earth. It would eat her alive knowing Middang3ard was a real place she could visit but wouldn't.

Then the gravity of the situation settled back in. The whole reason Myrddin needed Alex to come to Middang3ard was to fight in a war. A war meant people were dying. It meant there was a possibility she could die.

Alex thought back to all the times she'd seen her party members die. Those had been heart-wrenching moments, even with the knowledge that her friends were going to respawn a couple of hours later. Could she handle people actually dying?

Alex raised her hand as if she were in class. All the adults in the room stopped talking and looked at her. "People are dying in Middang3ard, aren't they?" Alex asked.

Myrddin solemnly nodded as he leaned forward on his cane. "Yes, they are, and most of them are innocent people. Our armies are well trained, as are our MERCs. We don't lose many of them, and we try not to send them into situations they aren't prepared for."

"Why is the Dark One doing this?"

"We've been trying to figure that out for years. There doesn't seem to be a reason. His backstory isn't known, unlike those of all the bosses we've included in your raids. We don't know why he decimates everything he comes in contact with."

Alex turned to her mother, resting her hand on Liza's kneecap. "Mom, it should be my choice."

Liza's eyes widened as she practically jumped from the sofa. "Like hell, it should be," Liza shouted as she shook her head vigorously. "The whole reason that…that this man is here is because he can't justify taking a child away from her parents."

Myrddin tapped his cane three times to get the room's

attention. "I am here because I care deeply about what is best for Alex. Just because I want her to come to Middang3ard does not mean I want her to fracture the relationships with those she is sworn to protect."

George was staring at the fireplace, where medals from his time in the Marines were displayed on the mantle. "Are you saying Alex has the potential to help people?" he asked. "To defend them? She isn't going to be some grunt you're throwing to the first infantry line or something like that?"

Liza threw her hands up in exasperation. "What does it matter?" she asked. "Either way, he's asking our daughter to risk her life for some world we know nothing about."

Myrddin raised his cane as if it would cast some kind of peace over the conversation. "I can assure you Alex would not be front-line fodder," he answered. "We are not the Army. Our Riders are highly trained and highly qualified. They are akin to the Navy SEALS and other such programs—"

Alex cut Myrddin off. "So, what am I to you?" she accused.

Myrddin did not back off from the question. "Our only hope, Obi-Wan," Myrddin replied.

Alex sighed.

"You think I'm joking, but no other humans have your reaction time. It rivals that of the elves in the Dragonrider program."

There was a brief silence before Liza and George started arguing with each other again. Alex tried to tune them out. She only caught an occasional word or phrase but was able to piece together what was going on regardless.

George thought they should hear Myrddin out. If Alex really was a prodigy and there really was a war going on, maybe it was their civic duty to let Alex make her own decision.

Liza wouldn't hear it. She didn't care if there was a war going on. She reminded George how adamant he'd been about never letting Alex join the Marines. Liza didn't see any difference simply because what Myrddin offered included dragons.

Alex stood up abruptly, causing both of her parents to stop talking. "How about we show them?" Alex stated. "We take them into Middang3ard and let them see the place I love so much for themselves."

For the first time since Myrddin had appeared in the room, he smiled. "That is a wonderful idea. What do the two of you think about it? You've seen screenshots, but they don't compare to the real thing. Step into my world and see what it is we are trying to protect."

Liza cast a dubious glance in Myrddin's direction. "You mean, you'll take us to Middang3ard?" she asked.

"Not the realm proper. Since humans have lost the use of magic, there are many protections we have in place to keep people from slipping in and out of Middang3ard. But allowing you to see the *Middang3ard* VR will give you a rough idea of what your daughter would be fighting for."

Alex could tell Liza still didn't trust Myrddin. Even though she'd only had a little bit of time to see her mother's reactions, Alex could already sense when her mother was not at ease.

George, on the other hand, could not have looked more excited. "Wait, you mean we can actually see it?" he asked. "And see Alex in action?"

Myrddin nodded as he stood. "You can definitely see the world, but I would advise against seeing Alex in action," he answered. "Your daughter's role in the game is somewhat dangerous. It is not for the faint of heart."

Alex shrugged and smiled as she stood and walked over

to Myrddin. "How about you let me take them out for a little bit?" she offered. "Give them my own kind of tour."

Myrddin waved his hand, and three VR sets appeared on the coffee table. "I would have it no other way." Myrddin chuckled. "Please show them a good time. You shouldn't have any problem adjusting your headsets. Put them on, and they'll take care of the rest."

Alex grabbed two of the headsets and handed them to her parents. She was eager to get started, and she saw that same eagerness was on her father's face. Liza did not look even remotely excited. "Come on, Mom. Give it a try," Alex encouraged.

Liza held the headset to her eyes and glared at the visor. "And you're saying this isn't dangerous?" she asked.

"Nope, not at all. I've been playing for months, and I've never had any problems."

"Fine. But if I don't like it, I'm going to log out. Understood?"

"Sounds fair enough."

Liza and George put on their headsets as Alex squeezed between them. She flashed Myrddin a thumbs-up before putting her own headset on. She hoped this would work. Who could go to *Middang3ard* and not fall in love with it?

Alex opened her eyes. She was sitting on a thatch bed back in *Middang3ard*. She looked around the room, checking to see if her parents had spawned where she had. When she leaned over and looked at the floor, she saw both of them. They had spawned in the fetal position. Alex waited for them to wake up.

Liza was the first to stir. She sat up, rubbing her eyes. When she saw Alex, there was no initial reaction. Then she smiled as if she'd just seen a long-lost friend. "Honey, your hair is so long," Liza gushed. "I've never seen you wear it that long before!"

Alex had forgotten that was the one thing she'd done to her appearance that didn't match up with real life. Since this was just a game, Alex went through three or four different options a week. She sometimes did quests just to unlock more styles; it was kind of a hobby.

"Oh, yeah," Alex shyly replied. "I was just curious. It's much easier to go to the hairstylist and see how something works here than have to spend three years growing my hair out, only to get a haircut I don't like. I have some pictures saved of the other ones in case you want to check them out."

Liza stood up and stretched while she looked around the room. "That sounds great," she said. "Is this your place? Do you have your own house?"

"No, no. I didn't want the whole house thing. I just have a room in a tavern."

"In a tavern?"

"Don't worry, Mom, it's not what you think. The taverns here are more like inns, and there's no alcohol for minors in the game. We just get a drink that makes our stomach warm, so you don't have to worry about that."

Liza looked down at George, who was still sleeping comfortably on the floor. "Is he okay?" she asked.

Alex knelt next to her father and nudged him with her finger. "Yeah, he's okay," she answered. "When you wake up in VR, it's a lot like waking up in real life. Some people are heavier sleepers than others. We could give him the ol' *Middang3ard* wakeup call if you want."

"What's that?"

Alex scrolled through her inventory until she found what she was looking for—a goblin war horn. She selected it, and the horn materialized in her hand, then she took a deep breath and blew with all she had.

George jumped up at the sound of the horn. His eyes went wide as he tried to find the source of the noise, and he looked as if he were likely to bolt out of the room from sheer fear.

Then he noticed Alex and Liza were laughing their butts off. "Ha-ha," George sarcastically muttered. "Mess with the guy who's enjoying a little nap. Real mature. Glad your sense of humor transfers to VR."

Alex walked a circle around her parents. Both George and Liza had spawned with basic peasant clothes. "You guys look kinda...blah," she said. "If we're going to go on a tour of *Middang3ard*, I don't want you two looking like a bunch of newbs. Let's get you some new clothes."

Alex went over to her closet and flung it open. This was where she kept all the armor she didn't want to lug around in her inventory. She figured it would be nice to hold onto in case she ever made another character or met a new player she wanted to help.

George leaned into the closet and whistled. "Wow, how come you can't manage to keep your room this clean?" he asked.

"My room is immaculate!" Alex retorted.

"How did you get so much cool stuff?"

"Different quests and shopping, I guess. My savings in *Middang3ard* makes the real-life me look like a pauper. Grab whatever you want, and make sure to pick a weapon, too. You never know what might reach out and grab you."

Liza didn't laugh at the joke, and Alex realized she might have to downplay how randomly dangerous *Middang3ard* could be, even if it was her favorite part. After waiting for her parents to choose their outfits, the trio left the room and went downstairs.

As usual, the tavern was mostly populated by dwarves and elves. There were a few humans and a handful of gnomes, but it looked like there might be an event going on in-game for elves and dwarves.

Either way, Liza and George could not keep their eyes in their heads. They gawked at every player who walked by, marveling at how realistic each race looked. "I used to play tabletop RPG games," Liza muttered. "I never saw any model or drawing that looked this good."

George bumped into a dwarf, nearly knocking his beer out of his hand. "Oh, I'm sorry," he apologized.

The dwarf puffed out his chest. "Oi, you better be, or we might have to settle this with axes," he barked.

Alex stepped between the dwarf and George. "Hey, hey, don't make this a bigger deal than it is," Alex threatened. "Or it'll be *my* axe you'll be tasting."

The dwarf looked Alex up and down, trying to gauge how big a threat the girl posed. "Hey, ain't you Boundless?" the dwarf asked.

Alex pretended not to be flattered by another player recognizing her, but if she was honest with herself, it was one of her favorite parts of *Middang3ard*. "In the virtual flesh," she finally admitted.

The dwarf's rough face broke into a smile. "Well, I'll be pickled. Word is you cleared the Dragonriders' expansion. Word's all over *Middang3ard*." The dwarf looked over his shoulder, then leaned in close to whisper, "Is it true what they say? About the invitation?"

Alex's eyes sparkled as she answered the dwarf. "Oh, it's true. I'm bringing my parents along for a little tour, so they can see what it's all about."

The dwarf turned to George and bowed low. "I apologize, good sir," the dwarf practically yelled. "I did not mean to insult the parents of Boundless. It is my honor to meet you.

She is one of the most honorable players I have had the plea-sure of raiding with. Good day to you, sir and milady!" The dwarf bowed again and strode off.

George and Liza gave Alex very impressed looks. "Do you usually get such a fanfare when you come here?" George asked.

Alex shrugged and pointed at the bar. "It's a *Middang3ard* custom to open a game with a cup of grog, or in your adult cases, a pint of ale before discussing the quests or plans for the day. You can even get food if you're hungry. I'd suggest it. The food here is amazing. Not quite as good as yours, Mom, but still pretty good."

The three of them went to the bar and ordered a grog, two ales, and a round of mutton cooked medium-rare. The barmaid brought the drinks, and Alex explained they were going to have to wait a little bit for their food. It was part of the VR immersion.

As George sipped his beer, he let out a sigh and said, "Well, I can tell you right now, I am thoroughly immersed."

After some time, the mutton came, and the three Bounds tore into the succulent meat. Liza took a break to talk to the barmaid about how the meat was prepared. She hadn't had anything so delicious before.

She wanted to take notes for George, who would not admit he was wowed until the meal was over. Finally, he leaned back in his chair, and exclaimed, "I can't believe this is virtual reality!"

Alex handed her cup back to the barmaid and polished off the last bit of mutton before standing. "You haven't even experienced the best part," Alex said. "Come on. Follow me."

Alex took her parents by the hands and pulled them from the tavern. It took everything she had not to go running down the village streets. She wanted to get them into the sky as soon as possible, but she also realized that much of what made *Middang3ard* interesting was its small intricacies.

The expertly-crafted town really did make you feel like you were in a completely different world. Alex made sure to walk slowly so her parents could absorb everything they saw.

George pointed at a metalworker's shop. "Can we go see the smith?" he asked.

Liza laughed as Alex directed them down the street. "George, you can see a blacksmith at a Renaissance fair," she said. "You don't have to use virtual reality for that."

They were nearing the edge of the village. Some of the local players and NPCs had recognized Alex and were gathering behind her to see her summon the dragon. Alex was beside herself with excitement. She knew this was going to blow her parents' minds.

Alex stepped into the clearing outside the village and turned back to her parents. "Don't freak out when you see this, all right?" she cautioned.

Liza folded her arms and nodded, her face smug and bemused. "We aren't going to freak out," Liza assured her daughter. "We aren't *that* old."

"Okay, I'll hold you to that."

Alex raised her right hand, and her Dragon Link glowed brightly. From above came the familiar roar that shook the roofs of the homes and buildings surrounding them. Liza and George threw themselves to the ground when they heard it.

"What the hell is that?" George shouted.

Alex smiled as she watched her dragon break through the clouds and race toward her. "*That*," Alex told them, pausing for effect, "is our ride."

The ether dragon hit the ground hard enough to shake the earth around it, gouging out a large crater. It spewed fire as it roared. The townsfolk went crazy, shouting and cheering with excitement when the dragon lowered its head and Alex leaped onto its back.

She anchored herself to the dragon and guided it toward her parents. They had gotten up but backed away as the dragon got closer. "Come on," Alex coaxed. "It's time for you two to see what I spend all my time doing."

The dragon put its head down so Liza and George could climb on. George went first, hands trembling as he reached out for his daughter's. He helped Liza get aboard once he was settled.

Alex waved her hand over both of her parents to anchor their feet to the dragon. "All right," Alex explained, "you're both going to need to relax. You can't fall, no matter what. Doesn't matter how fast we're going or if we turn upside-down. Just enjoy the ride, okay?"

Liza frantically looked from her daughter to George, and then at the sky. "Wait, you're not telling me you're planning on taking us up there, are you?" she yelped.

"Like I said, you two are going to need to relax."

Alex tightened the reins, and the dragon responded to her command. It spread its mighty wings and flapped them, slowly rising into the air. Usually, Alex would have just rocketed into the sky, but she wanted to give her parents a little space to catch their breath.

She was glad she did because Liza and George were practically screaming as the dragon rose higher and higher. *Either way, they're going to freak out*, Alex thought. *Might as well give them something to scream about.*

Alex pulled back on her Dragon Link and her ether dragon shot up into the sky so fast it brought tears to Alex's eyes. The screams of her parents grew louder and louder, until finally they burst through the first layer of clouds.

The dragon slowed, almost floating in the air.

The sun filtered through the clouds, painting everything

in a golden hue. From here, it was smooth sailing. The dragon soared above the village beneath them. "This," Alex said, "this is what I spend all of my time doing. But this? This isn't nothing."

Alex leaned forward, and the ether dragon sped up like a shooting star. They were headed east. There was something Alex wanted to show her parents—her favorite place. She'd never shared it with anyone else in *Middang3ard*.

Alex wasn't even sure other players knew about it. This area of the map was hardly ever explored since there were so many high-level monsters on the ground. But Dragonriders? They could go anywhere.

They flew in silence for some time. Liza and George had finally relaxed and were watching the clouds pass. They were beyond words. Alex knew how they felt; it had been the same for her.

Alex could never sum up how it felt to stare down at the world of *Middang3ard* and see how small and fragile everything was. She didn't think she would ever get tired of it.

Finally, they came up on what Alex wanted to show them. It was a mountain, nearly as large as the one during the final expansion raid. Its peak was covered in snow.

Alex leaned forward to coax the dragon ahead. A few minutes later, they were at the top of the mountain. She guided her dragon to a landing area and leaped off before telling her parents they could do the same.

The Bounds walked across the snow-covered ground. Alex went to the edge of the mountain and sat down, dangling her feet over. Liza sat down next to her, while George stood behind them. "So, this is what you want to protect?" Liza asked.

Alex didn't say anything at first. It was more than a want. "This is what I *have* to protect," she finally replied.

A voice came from behind them. "What do you think of *Middang3ard?*"

Liza and George turned and were greeted by another holograph of Myrddin. Liza looked down at the sweeping green plains, the villages, and all the people not even visible from this height.

Above them, youngling dragons were playing with each other and dancing in the sunlight. "It's beautiful," Liza admitted. "And it's real?"

"Just as real and fragile as Earth."

Liza sat back down at Alex's side. "Honey, what do you want to do?" she asked.

"You mean it?" Alex replied.

Her mother took a long moment before finally nodding, wiping away her tears. "There's nothing I can say to stop you."

"It's the right thing to do."

Liza nodded, gulping back more tears. "This is your decision, not ours. Not mine. Whatever you decide, we'll support you."

Alex watched the dragons dancing above as she leaned back in the snow so she could feel the cold creep up the back of her neck. "I want to be able to talk to them every day, no matter what. Anytime I want to."

Myrddin came over and took a seat next to the Bounds. "Of course," Myrddin offered. "Unlimited communication is the least we can do for our champions."

Alex's face lit up with a smile as she turned to face Myrddin.

"Awesome. When do we leave?"

The story is far from over.
The battle continues in Ascent to the Nest!

It's Christmas, people... and here in the Vance household we have a tradition... we sing 'Hi John'.

Sure we *also* sing Christmas carols, carve turkey and wear sweat pants, but it wouldn't be Christmas without 'Hi John'.

John (my four year old at the time of this publication) was born 5 weeks early in one of the most harrowing 20 minutes of my life. My wife had developed a condition called H.E.L.L.P. (ironic name, I know). It is incredibly dangerous for the mother and she needed to have an emergency cesarean.

Over the next 6 days, I spend my time divided between the post-natal ward with John and the 'blood ward' (my name for the place) where my wife was being treated.

So here I was, alone with a new born that I had no idea what to do with. Hell, I didn't even know any nursery rhymes or songs. My wife knew them all, but she was in another ward, completely out of it.

John would cry and I wouldn't know what to do (even writing this induces the water-works... hold yourself Ramy! You're in a very crowded cafe. Stiff upper lip. Stiff upper lip!)

Eventually I did the only thing I could think of … I made a song up. Now if you've ever met me, you'll know that I have zero musical talent. Seriously. I mean, I've heard about the 'beat'. People have told me it exists, but I've never experienced it for myself.

And the little diddy I made up for my son reflects that… Here are the lyrics:

Hi John, how are you?
How are you, today?
I love John so much,
I love him more than play...
Hi, John, how are you?
What shall we do today?

Rudimentary, right? But here's the weird thing. My son would stop crying as soon as I sang: *I love him more than play...*

When he hears those words, he's go silent.

Every. Single. Time.

In the coming years, I have convinced people I know to professionally record the song. I got country-and-western singer named Steve Rivers to do it, a Norweigen Rock Band and a Hip Hop Producer, too. (If you'd like to check out the various versions of the song, they're all in my Facebook Group: House of the GoneGod Damned. Click HERE to join. I'll be sharing a post about the song on Chrismas Day, 2019.)

And so now, several different versions of 'Hi John' later, a new Christmas tradition is born.

A song for John, the kid I truly love more than anything, even play...

AUTHOR NOTES MICHAEL ANDERLE
DECEMBER 21, 2019

Thank you for reading our story! Because of you readers, we get to do what we love...create more stories!

"Blind? We are going to do a blind hero? *AND* you want to..."

You know, I don't really remember the exact way Ramy and I worked out this story.

Not without going back through our notes, where we chatted back and forth, but I am very happy with this first book. In it, we lay out the challenges of our protagonist and how she has to overcome her preconceptions about *herself*.

And she's then unleashed into her future.

The more I learn about my own disability (I'm a bit on the spectrum), I realize that had I known more about it earlier in my life, I might have sought out ways to overcome the challenges. However, I am completely happy with the unexpected benefits.

Yes, I am challenged at times working with other people because I fail to communicate well. I've had issues talking to everyone from my older brothers to workmates because my brain fails to put into words all of my thoughts in a cohesive discourse.

When I see nothing but confusion on the faces of those I'm speaking to, I know I have once again left out a few salient points.

But unleash me with a laptop, and the challenges I have talking to others go away. I can't explain a story while chatting at the table, but I can weave a tale with a typewriter.

For all the challenges which often cause failure when speaking, I'm provided benefits when I type. What I would have sacrificed to "fix" earlier in my life, I wouldn't give a dime to change now. What felt like a curse, I now count as a blessing.

May you find how what you feel is a curse might become a blessing to you as well.

Ad Aeternitatem,

Michael Anderle

OTHER BOOKS BY THE AUTHORS

Other Middang3ard Books

Never Split The Party (01)
Late To the Party (02)
It's My Party (03)

Death Of An Author: A Middang3ard Novella

Other Books by Ramy Vance

Mortality Bites Series
Keep Evolving Series
Fatebound Series

Other Books by Michael Anderle

For a complete list of books by Michael Anderle, please visit:

www.lmbpn.com/ma-books/

All LMBPN Audiobooks are Available at Audible.com and iTunes. To see all LMBPN audiobooks, including those written by Michael Anderle please visit:

www.lmbpn.com/audible

CONNECT WITH THE AUTHORS

Connect with Ramy

Join Ramy's Newsletter

Join Ramy's FB Group: House of the GoneGod Damned!

Connect with Michael Anderle and sign up for his email list here:

Website: http://lmbpn.com

Email List: http://lmbpn.com/email/

Facebook:
www.facebook.com/TheKurtherianGambitBooks

www.ingramcontent.com/pod-product-compliance
Lightning Source LLC
Chambersburg PA
CBHW050157110726
47898CB00008B/2845